LOOKIN' GOOD,
BEETLE BAILEY

Here's another in the happy series of books based
on one of the most famous comic strips in the
country. Once again the madcap inmates of
Camp Swampy valiantly strive to overcome their
own ineptitude—and succeed in delighting us on
every page.

Mort Walker again gives us a barrel of laughs in
his marvelous cartoons concerning the most un-
professional soldier in the army!

Lookin' Good,
beetle bailey®

Mort Walker

TEMPO BOOKS, NEW YORK

LOOKIN' GOOD, BEETLE BAILEY

A Tempo Book / published by arrangement with
King Features Syndicate, Inc.

PRINTING HISTORY
Tempo edition / June 1977
Fifth printing / July 1983

ISBN: 0-441-05318-1

Tempo Books are published by Charter Communications, Inc.,
200 Madison Avenue, New York, New York 10016.
Tempo Books are registered in the United States Patent Office.
PRINTED IN THE UNITED STATES OF AMERICA

12-1

DON'T GO RUNNING WITH THOSE FRIENDS OF YOURS, OR YOU'LL GET PICKED UP

12-8

IS HE RUNNING WITH A WILD PACK?

I DON'T KNOW HOW WILD THEY ARE...

BUT THEY SURE LOOK SHIFTY

MORT WALKER

I MUST BE GETTING OLD. **EVERYTHING** ACHES!

GO SOAK IN A HOT TUB

1-22

I GUESS THAT'S ONE WAY TO GET AT ALL MY ACHES AT ONCE

MARTHA! HAVE YOU SEEN MY SNORKEL?

FIGHT WITH MY WIFE

GENERAL! YOU SHOULDN'T LET HER DO THAT TO YOU!

1-25

I DIDN'T **LET** HER

MORT WALKER

MY BOBBING AND WEAVING AND HEAD FAKES JUST AREN'T WHAT THEY USED TO BE

Dear Diary!
there is a woman on the post that we will have to do something about.

the men cannot deal with her presence in a rational manner. the mere sight of her makes them tremble.

3-3

Her name is

Mrs Bugley!

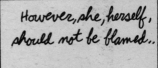

However, she, herself, should not be blamed...

MORT WALKER

© King Features Syndicate, Inc., 1977.